Hello, there!
Welcome to my UNLUCKY book.
I've had some trouble with it,
as you can see.
That's a squashed fly down there.

And yet, it all began so well.

For Colette, Lylah and Phoebe – A.A.

For Ramona, Alvie and Ted – B.I.

My Worst Book Ever! © 2018 Thames & Hudson Ltd, London
Text © 2018 Allan Ahlberg
Illustration © 2018 Bruce Ingman

First published in hardback in the United States of America by
Thames & Hudson Inc., 500 Fifth Avenue, New York, New York 10110

www.thamesandhudsonusa.com

Library of Congress Control Number 2017945804

ISBN 978-0-500-65090-5

Printed and bound in China by Toppan Leefung Printing Limited

Disclaimer: no flies were harmed in the making of this book.

MY WORST BOOK EVER!

by *Allan Ahlberg*

with pictures by *Bruce Ingman*

Thames & Hudson

Yes, it all began so well.
There was I down in my writing shed:
early morning, cup of coffee,
blank page, *teeming* brain.

I had this promising story—
CROCODILE SNAP!—all about a family:
little boy, older girl, baby, mom and dad,
and a *desperate*, CRAFTY, s n e a k i n g

. . . crocodile.

Little ducks dreaming
Afternoon nap
Riverbank steaming
Crocodile...
Snap!

Ha, ha! Yes, you can see it, can't you?
That brave little chap . . .

Billy Brown boating
Brave little chap
Crocodile floating
Crocodile ... snap!

I was happy—joyful!—doing the work I was born to do.
Then, hardly had I put my cup down and picked
my pencil up, when the door flew open,
the cat flew in, and the *coffee* went—
you guessed it—f l y i *n* g.

Look at it! What a mess—and paw marks too.
There was a fox, would you believe it,
a *fox* in the garden, chasing the cat.

oh dear

Billy Brown boating
Brave little chap
Crocodile floating
Crocodile ... Snap!

So I mopped things up, carried the cat
back into the house, ignored the phone,
got another cup of coffee, *fed* the cat
and returned to my shed.

Where was I? Hm . . . brave little chap.
I liked this story. I was beginning to
see the shape of it: the family, the ducks,
how the crocodile could . . . Hm.

BOUR
Crocodile creeping
Finds a gap (in the fence)
Mr Brown sleeping*
Crocodile . . . Snap!
*Yes, we'll have Mr Brown in a hammock, I think

I sipped my coffee, leant back in my chair
and gazed out at the sunny garden.
I gave some thought to the
behavior of the crocodile,
his s n e a k y eyes,
his SNAPPING jaws . . .

Mrs Brown singing
Baby on lap
Back door swinging*
Crocodile ... Snap!

*(I like that line. It's mysterious, isn't it? Menacing)

I made a list of useful
(and not so useful)
"snap" rhymes.

trap flap mousetrap
map bap watch strap
slap map bubble wrap
cap hubcap Toule Sap
(Cambodian Lake)
yap Kneecap wendletrap
(marine mollusc)

Only then—Oh no, not again!—
the door flew open
and my wife and children,
      with their luggage,
      sunhats,
      buckets and spades,
      came bursting in.

We had a vacation booked.
Oh dear, and I had quite forgotten it.

So off we went,
all five of us,
in our crowded car
to the seaside . . .

for a w h o l e week.

On holidays I am not supposed to work.
I have to enjoy myself,
and I do—I really do.
Sandcastles. Donkey rides. Crazy golf.
Oh yes, great fun.

Then, one week later, back home . . .

to our happy cat,
cosy house,
cup of coffee . . .

and shed.

And what do I find?
My book's been EATEN—
holes all over it—

LOOK!

Mrs Brown singing
Baby on lap
ack door swinging
Crocodile Snap!

My *unlucky* book
    —squashed flies!
    —coffee!
    —and vandalism!

Guess what did it. Go on!
Bet you can't.

SNAILS.

Mrs Bro~~wn~~

Baby on

~~b~~ack door

Crocodile

Snails from the garden
crept in under the door,

climbed onto the desk

singing

lap

singing

Snap!

and *ate my story.*
(Snails eat paper, y'know.)

There again, I was into this story now
and nothing could stop me.
Quick as a flash, I tossed those greedy snails
out the window, drank some refreshing coffee
and wrote two more verses.

Hall clock chiming
Little dog, Yap!
Crocodile climbing
Crocodile... Snap!

Sally Brown humming
Shower and cap
Crocodile coming
Crocodile... Snap!
(Yes, yes, he's in the house now,
on the stairs!)

Phew! I could *feel* the tension.
I was gripping my pencil so hard
I had to go up to the house
and have a chocolate biscuit
to calm me down.
Watch a bit of T.V.
Play with the cat.

Then, later that evening
when the children were in bed,
I brought my work to the kitchen table,
took a firm hold of that story
and *finished* it.

After which I wrote my favorite
two words in all the world,

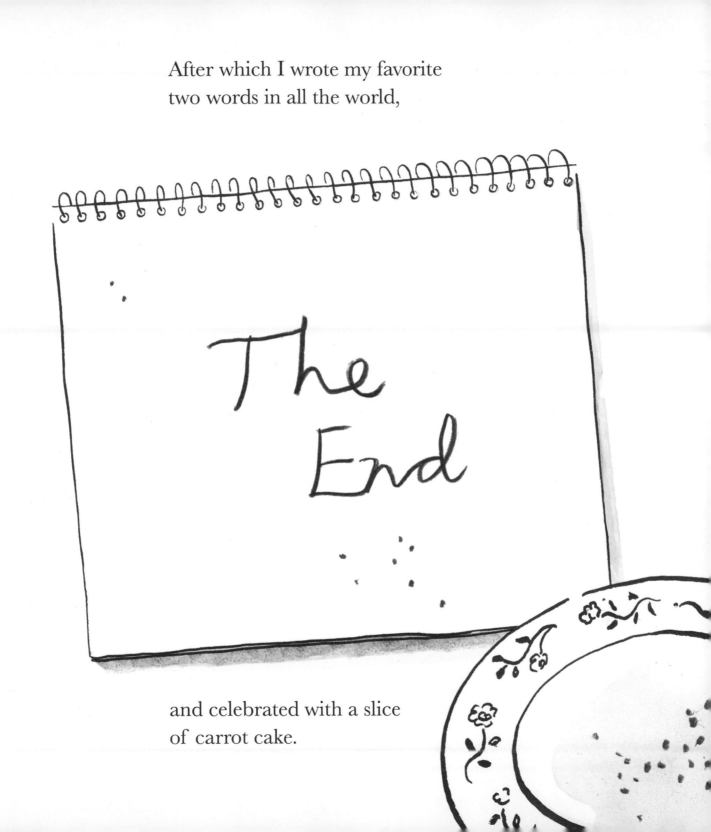

and celebrated with a slice
of carrot cake.

Only it wasn't, of course, "The End."
This book was a picture book.
Picture books need pictures,
and I needed Bruce.

Bruce is a good friend
and an even better illustrator.
He's amazing.
He can draw and color his pictures
almost as fast as I can write.

Anyway, he lived nearby, so the next day
I went around to see him.
He read the story.
"I love it!" he said.
"Crocodiles!" he said.
"My favorite!" he said.

Two days later *he* came round to see *me*,
with a pile of pictures under his arm.
He had illustrated half the book.
    My heart was leaping inside me.
I could not wait to see them.

"There are a couple of little changes," said Bruce.
I looked at the pictures. Have a look yourself.
See if—in a book entitled "Crocodile Snap!"—
you can spot the deliberate mistake.

Yes, you got it—

NO crocodile!

"What's this?" I said
"A hippopotamus," said Bruce.
"A hippopotamus?" said I.
"Yes," said Bruce.
"There're too many crocodile books.
A hippopotamus is more original."

At that moment—as my heart was sinking—
the door flew open—Again!—and in came
a muscular little boy named Ted,
Bruce's youngest child.

He was followed by
all three of my children,
who had been entertaining him
in the garden.
The whole gang of them
crowded into the shed.

Ted somehow got himself
onto the desk
and out the window,
dribbling his raspberry lolly
all over his daddy's precious artwork
and leaving his sticky handprints . . .

everywhere.

Bruce and Ted finally went home.
Bruce promised to get rid of the hippo.
A week later the two of us caught a train to New York.
Picture books need pictures—yes.
They also need . . .

a publisher.

Bruce and I sat in the publisher's office
and showed the book to our editor.

"I love it!" she said.

"Crocodiles!" she said.

"My favorite!" she said.

Then she got excited and wanted to swap
the crocodile for a dinosaur.

Bruce got excited and did some dinosaur pictures.

I got excited and said

"No! No!
No! No! NO!
NO!

NO!"

Then the designer came in and he got excited about . . .

. . . fonts.

SNAP!

Billy Brown boating
Brave little chap
Crocodile floating
Crocodile . . .

SNAP!

Billy Brown boating
Brave little chap
Crocodile floating
Crocodile . . .

SNAP!

Billy Brown boating
Brave little chap
Crocodile floating
Crocodile . . .

Anyway, musn't grumble.
That's how a book gets made, after all.
Teamwork.
We sorted it out — no hippos,
no dinosaurs, no fancy fonts.

Bruce and I went home to our cosy homes
and sheds and our loving families.

The book went off to the printer.

Whereupon—you guessed it—

MORE

trouble.

It turned out the printer
had a little girl too,
a four-year-old named Lucy.

Lucy was always on the go,
and loved to help her daddy.
Those are her (chocolatey)
handprints down there.

Lucy "tidied up" the pages.

To save paper, Bruce had drawn some hippos
and dinosaurs on the back of his crocodile pictures.
Lucy tidied them up as well, along with some pages
in other languages. A couple of font samples also crept in.

Yes, the whole lot of it, all bundled up into one

perfectly N E A T and T I D Y...

mish-mash.

So here we are, close now to the

CATASTROPHE.

Let me show you, shall I?
Have a look under this flap.
This is how my book should have been.
A pleasant enough tale,
as you can see.
Not Roald Dahl, of course,
or Julia Donaldson even, but not bad.

CROCODILE SNAP!

Allan Ahlberg · Bruce Ingman

(p.t.o.)

Whereas here—under this flap—
is what the printer actually printed,
and the publisher actually posted to me
—oh dear!—in a jiffy bag.
MY WORST BOOK EVER.

CROCODILE SNAP!

Allan Ahlberg · Bruce Ingman

(p.t.o.)

Well, as you can imagine,
I was pretty sad after that.
Inconsolable.
For a whole week I sat in my shed:
blunt pencil, blank page,
blank brain. Oh dear.

Only then, one sunny summer's morning
sipping my coffee and gazing around,
I had an idea.

SPIDERS ON THE MARCH!

One sunny summer's morning
A little boy named Paul
Found a teeny tiny spider
With a hat on in the hall

He followed it into the
garden

The spider's name was Horace
He was scuttling off to meet
His special pal, named Shirley
Who lived just down the street.

Shirley was a bit . . . bigger

Ha, ha, yes! You can see them, can't you?
Those spiders—hats, boots, rucksacks.
Getting bigger all the time.
On the march!

Oh yes, I was happy again—joyful!—
doing the work I was born to do.
It was going to be all right, this time,
I could tell.

After all, what could possibly . . .

. . . go wrong?